Funny Hunny Christmas

By Ann Braybrooks
Cover illustration by Costa Alavezos
Interior illustrations by Josie Yee

A Random House PICTUREBACK® Book
Random House 🏠 New York

Copyright © 2000, 2003 by Disney Enterprises, Inc. Based on the "Winnie the Pooh" stories by A. A. Milne and E. H. Shepard.
All rights reserved under International and Pan-American Copyright Conventions. Published in the United States by Random House Children's Books,
a division of Random House, Inc., New York, and simultaneously in Canada by Random House of Canada Limited, Toronto, in conjunction with Disney
Enterprises, Inc. Originally published in slightly different form by Golden Books Publishing Company, Inc., in 2000 as *The Sweetest Christmas*.
Library of Congress Control Number: 2001091681   ISBN: 0-7364-1328-6
www.randomhouse.com/kids/disney
Printed in the United States of America   10 9 8 7 6 5 4 3 2 1
PICTUREBACK, RANDOM HOUSE, and the Random House colophon are registered trademarks of Random House, Inc.

One Christmas Eve, Pooh stood at the window, staring out at the falling snow.

"Oh, bother!" he muttered. "Now I can't go outside to find presents for my friends."

"Think, think, think," said Pooh to himself. "I know, I shall look inside."

Under his bed Pooh found a box. "Yo-yos would make nice Christmas presents, but I suppose they would be more useful if they had strings."

Next, Pooh found some pinwheels in a drawer.
He blew on one pinwheel after another, but for some
reason none of them would spin.

"The wind must have worn these pinwheels out,"
he said.

Then Pooh noticed some marbles in a jar.

"I have eight friends," Pooh said happily to himself, "so I shall need eight marbles. One, two, three . . . four, five, six. Six? Oh, stuff and fluff. I don't have enough."

Pooh slumped in a chair. "Think, think, think,"
he said. "What would *I* want for Christmas?"
　　Just then Pooh's tummy rumbled. "I know!"
he cried. "HONEY!"

Pooh hurried to his cupboard and counted his honeypots. "Eight," he said, frowning, "which means there wouldn't be any left for me."

Pooh thought and thought. Finally he declared, "I do want to give my friends something wonderful. So honey it must be."

Pooh waited for the snow to stop falling. Then he loaded all eight honeypots onto his sled and headed for Piglet's house.

When Piglet opened the door, Pooh handed him a pot of honey. "Merry Christmas, Piglet!" cried Pooh.

"Merry Christmas, Pooh!" replied Piglet. And he handed Pooh a gift, too.

At Owl's, Pooh delivered another pot of honey. "Merry Christmas, Owl!" said Pooh.

"Merry Christmas, Pooh!" said Owl. "I have a present for you, too. My aunt Beazy—Beatrice, that is—collected it last spring."

"Why, thank you, Owl!" Pooh said politely. Then he hurried on to see Rabbit.

Next, Pooh gave Rabbit a pot of honey, and Rabbit gave Pooh a gift in return.

"Oh, Rabbit," cried Pooh. "You shouldn't have!"

"Oh, yes, I should," grumbled Rabbit. "Now maybe you won't eat mine!"

Then Eeyore and Pooh exchanged presents.

"Fancy that," said Eeyore. "One for me, and one for you. I'm going to have this honey with thistles. Thank you, Pooh."

Pooh headed for Kanga's house.

On the way he ran into Christopher Robin.
"I'm delivering Christmas presents to my friends,"
Pooh told him, "but I had to use up all my honey."
"Oh, Pooh!" said Christopher Robin. "I have a wonderful
idea. You go on to Kanga's, and I'll see you soon."

When Pooh arrived at Kanga's house, he found Tigger
with Kanga and Roo.
"Merry Christmas, everyone!" said Pooh.

While Pooh was giving his friends their pots of honey, Christopher Robin hurried in with a large box.

"Tigger, Kanga, and Roo have something for you, Pooh," said the boy. "Why don't you open all your presents now?"

Pooh's surprise grew as he unwrapped one pot of honey after another. Finally he opened the large box from Christopher Robin. Inside were five more honeypots!

"Merry Christmas, Pooh!" said Christopher Robin. "You've been such a kind and generous bear that you deserve pots and pots of honey!"

"Oh, thank you!" exclaimed Pooh as he helped himself to a smackerel. "Mmm," he said, licking his lips. "What a very sweet Christmas this is!"